CW00818950

SPACE   E
E
REARVIEW MIRRORS

50-WORD STORIES

RAN WALKER

ALTERNATE
45
PRESS

© 2023 Randolph Walker, Jr.
All rights reserved.
Cover image used courtesy of Strvnge Films

ISBN: 9781020001383 (Paperback)
ISBN: 9781020001390 (Ebook)
Library of Congress Control Number: 2023901457

First Edition
10 9 8 7 6 5 4 3 2

45 Alternate Press, LLC
Hampton, VA

CONTENTS

For those who create small

PREFACE

It's been two years since I wrote my first collection of 50-word stories, *The Strange Museum*. This was my first foray into microfiction, proof to myself that I could not only write in the form, but also become somewhat prolific with it. Afterwards, I shifted to writing 100-word stories, writing six books of them, before looking back at the form that kicked off my entire microfiction experience.

Frankly, I wondered if I could still write them after having twice as many words to play with for a while. Thanks to Tim Sevenhuyen, editor of *50-Word Stories*, I was able to read hundreds of 50-words stories written by writers from all over the world. Reading their work inspired me, and the itch to contribute to this space returned with a vengeance.

The process of writing these stories was not identical to that of the 100-word story process, but it was fun to further distill my ideas to their bare bones, pushing to pack as much into fifty words as I could.

I sincerely hope you enjoy this collection as much

as I enjoyed writing it. And who knows? Maybe there will be another collection in the future.

Best,

Ran

I'll give you the whole secret to short story writing. Here it is. Rule 1: Write stories that please yourself. There is no Rule 2.

O. HENRY

PART 1

1

HOW TO BECOME LEGENDARY

FIRST YOU DIE. Then they make a t-shirt of you. If you're lucky, they'll sell it at a Hot Topic or a Spencer's in the mall, alongside other dead rappers, all of whom died far too young, and maybe, just maybe, someone other than a family member will buy one.

MY GIRLFRIEND, THE ACTRESS

SECRETLY, my girlfriend wants to be an actress. I can tell by the way she moves around, flourishing her hands when she talks, and the way she delivers her monologue about planning to leave me for a man with more going for him. Personally, I think the script needs work.

3

THE CRUCIVERBALIST

HE'S NEVER DONE a *New York Times* crossword puzzle in ink. That would be pretentious. Solving one is an art, and that has little to do with performance. It's about understanding the right clues and filling in the rest. He has come to realize this is a lot like life.

4

SEEDS

HE'S GROWING A NIGHTMARE GARDEN. When he's startled awake in the middle of the night, he runs to the plot in his backyard and screams into a fresh hole, covering it up. He has planted many seeds, but no fruit has emerged from the soil. Maybe that's for the best.

EUPHONIC CACOPHONY

THE JAZZ TRIO played louder to cover the screams of the people in the streets. The doors were locked and chained. They'd be safe inside for a while. And rather than fear the inevitable, they chose to continue playing the best set of their lives, making the screams their melody.

6

TRICK OR TREAT

THE KIDS relentlessly knocked on the door, their extravagant costumes glowing beneath the porch light. Alice looked at the empty candy bowl in the foyer and rubbed her sweaty hands against her jeans. The empty bowl was the least of her problems. She was more concerned because it was July.

THE NEIGHBOR

HE WROTE about them all the time in his fiction, horror stories filled with husband-slaughtering wives and wild teenagers wielding bats on the elderly. In the years after his death, his neighbors were surprised to learn of his hobby, all of them having thought he was the friendliest of neighbors.

ABLE TO LEAP TALL INSECURITIES
IN A SINGLE BOUND

SHE'D BEEN able to fly for quite some time now. She no longer needed to run before take off and didn't require props like capes either. Still, she kept this secret to herself. Her boyfriend was already insecure that she made more money than he. This certainly wouldn't help matters.

DAY 701 OF THE PANDEMIC

IT TOOK her weeks to convince him he could now take her out to dinner. She'd even bought him a new suit for the occasion. But now there was that booger in his nose. She wanted to tell him, but she feared it might completely undo all of their progress.

PLEASE DON'T SLAP THE PICASSO
FOR DW

THE SIGN in front of the large sculpture read "Please Don't Slap the Picasso." It was the kind of sign that clearly indicated someone had done the very thing for which everyone was now being banned.

I stared at the sculpture and couldn't help wondering how slapping it must've felt.

NIGHT LANDING

THEY LAY ON THEIR BACKS, the darkness around them a shared blanket, the fan revolving casually, as if this were normal, as if they hadn't just met at the airport and shared a cab—here. But the city was like that: bringing two lonely people together for moments so fleeting.

THE OCTOGENARIAN

SHE STARTED WRITING SHORTLY after her eightieth birthday. In the ten years that followed, she published thirty books, many of them far better than anyone had expected. Literature professors pointed to her as some kind of anomaly, but those who knew her best understood she had always been a writer.

A LIFE IN THE LIFE OF AN ACTOR

HER IMDB PAGE was full of tiny roles, many of them non-speaking, where she played different ethnicities, never her own, at ages she had long surpassed, but a job was a job, and there was always the possibility that a producer would spot her and give her her big break.

THE LAST SNOWFLAKE

IDEAS WERE LIKE SNOWFLAKES, he figured. All he needed to do was reach out and take one. But even as he did, they began to feel finite, and he suspected one day he'd run out of ideas, even though there were still millions of them gently circling all around him.

THE LOST AND FOUND

SHE FOUND the notebook in the lost and found and had considered leaving it for its owner to possibly discover one day. But she couldn't resist.

She took it home and read every word, living in the author's world for several days. When she was finished, she quietly returned it.

16

THE GAMER

SHE SPENT all afternoon practicing combinations on her new video game controller. By the following day, she'd learned how to make her boyfriend get off the couch, mow the yard, and even trim the hedges. With a little effort, maybe she'd get him to start putting the toilet seat down.

COTTON CANDY CLOUDS

AT NIGHT, her mother put her to bed by telling her stories of cotton candy clouds and a winged unicorn named Percival. She dreamed she was flying on Percival, occasionally trotting along various rainbows. Heaven couldn't be that far away, she figured. She could sense her father waving to her.

18

MAMA-SAN

MAMA-SAN WASN'T ACTUALLY A MOTHER, but, in a way, we were all her children. The gangs refused to sell her protection for her laundry mat, declaring her place neutral ground, and in return, she posted copies of their kids' report cards in the window when they made the honor roll.

MEN IN MOURNING

TERRELL DIDN'T BOTHER CHANGING out of his work shirt. Sitting down, he placed the Budweiser six-pack on the table between Grandpa and himself. Grandma had been gone a year. The beer and conversation was a poor substitute for hugs and peach cobbler, but the men did the best they could.

THE FUNAMBULIST

THERE WERE certain words she couldn't use around him, certain mannerisms she had to restrict herself from doing. Everything had to be done just so, a perfection that lived in his mind, one she couldn't comprehend.

But she would never leave him. She could handle this tightrope better than loneliness.

21

LA VOYEUSE

SHE WAS ALWAYS WATCHING, and when she wasn't watching, she was writing about watching: people moving about their lives in curious ways, everything a mystery, each word an attempt to qualify what her eyes had seen, make sense of it all, help her better understand her place in it all.

THE BIBLIOPHILE

HE WOULD SOMETIMES SLEEP with his books, several outlining his body, others resting beneath his pillows. He loved holding them, tracing his fingers along their covers. And while this should have been enough to inspire him to learn to read, he was content to collect them for their beauty alone.

23

FLYING SAUCERS

IN THEIR SPARE TIME, they gazed at the clouds, hoping to catch sight of a flying saucer while they sipped on their beers. Theopholis Nance had claimed he'd been abducted and returned to his backyard, no worse for the wear.

"Those anal probes," he remarked with sincerity, "were oddly satisfying."

24

NATSU

SHE ENJOYS CURLING up on the sofa, listening to the Hatsune Hirakura Trio while reading Haruki Murakami beneath her Spirited Away blanket. Outside her brownstone, she hears Biggie's thick flow emerging from rolled-down car windows. She smiles. It's summer in Brooklyn. She wonders what summer would be like in Japan.

25

INK

HE DOUBTED they'd take him seriously if he didn't have any tattoos. All the other rappers had tattoos—even on their faces. His mother told him Tupac was once viewed as having had too many tattoos on his body. He wondered what Tupac would think of all this ink now.

DIALOGUE OF A FIRST DATE

"Are you an Elvis fan?"

"I liked him when he was younger. I didn't really like the older Elvis as much."

"You mean Fat Elvis?"

"He wasn't fat. That was the steroids. They made him swollen."

"Swollen?"

"Yep. Swollen."

"So I should call him Swollen Elvis then."

"Yes."

"Swollen Elvis."

27

THE "S" WORD

TIRED OF NEGOTIATING reparations with descendants of the nation's formerly enslaved people, the government abruptly ceased discussion and issued money in the exact amounts of the original purchases, sans inflation, and issued them on the original defunct Southern currency the government had never backed, and considered the matter officially closed.

28

PURPLE
A POLITICAL STORY

WE'RE like leaves blowing in the wind. Some years I win; other years she wins. I try not to hate when she wins, choosing instead to remain focused on when my turn comes around. We simply cross our fingers hoping the other doesn't cause too much damage in the meantime.

29
___

BEAUFORT
FOR TMA AND JA

THEY HAD the kind of love that camped out in cotton shirts, damp with perspiration from morning gardening, afternoon lovemaking, evenings with her back pressed against his chest, as they looked into an endless sky and pondered how the love they shared felt bigger than the entire universe before them.

THE FIRST BOOK

THE BOOK FELL out of him in a clump, fully formed, perfect (if there were such a thing), its complexities dripping from each page. He stared at it, still covered in vomit like vernix caseosa on a newborn, amazed that his body could, from its depths, produce such a thing.

THE ENTERTAINER

HE DANCED and sang and everyone applauded him. His talent brought them immeasurable joy, making them forget their problems.

But he was deeply unhappy, fearing what they would think of him if he stopped. So he continued singing and dancing.

When he finally died, they gave him a standing ovation.

32

EXTINGUISHED

THE FIRST TIME they held hands, there was a spark. They both felt it and fell in love with it. But each time after that when their hands touched, there was less and less of that spark until finally it ceased completely. Eventually neither could remember that feeling at all.

33

SPACESHIPS DON'T COME EQUIPPED WITH REARVIEW MIRRORS

HE WOULDN'T HAVE KNOWN about it had his mother not called him and shared the news.

"It was in the lifestyle section this morning."

He wrestled with the idea Angie was getting married. His mother took no delight in telling him.

Slowly, he realized Angie had been enough all along.

THE DUDE BEHIND THE MASK

THEY STOOD there clothed in merch, an ocean of fans looking to be rocked by the greatest underground MC to ever do it. Then the masked imposter took the stage. Thirty pounds lighter, no scraggly beard, no Dumile.

Only a dastardly villain could do something like this to his fans.

AFRICAN-AMERICAN FEATURE-LENGTH ANIMATION

SHE DIDN'T SMILE for the sake of smiling or to make others feel at ease around her—not anymore. That mask lay forever cracked on the floor of her mind. She'd watched her son shrink himself, but he was never small enough to avoid detection by those who feared him.

HOW TO WRITE A 50-WORD STORY

Elisha had inquired how one could write a story using only fifty words. She received a variety of answers, some useful, others not so much. The one that resonated with her the most, though, was this: find the square root of the idea that is your story and write that.

SLOW TIMES AT DAILY HIGH, CIRCA 1992

THE LETTER RESTED at the bottom of his backpack. He'd stayed up the previous night, listening to SWV, writing in his best penmanship, sealing it with a mist of Cool Water.

He planned to give the letter to her between classes. Whatever happened after that was strictly up to her.

THE FAR SIDE, OR 12 THE HARD WAY

AFTER THE PHARCYDE

HE COULDN'T STOP DREAMING about Gary's mother wearing bright red boxers and beatboxing behind Lou Rawls. It was almost poetic, if it weren't originally intended to be an insult.

What if all of the dozen disses became real? Would his mother really be outside ironing her drawers in the driveway?

REJECTION

DEAR WRITER:

I am away from my desk for the next two weeks. To make matters quicker and more efficient, I am notifying you that while I've not had the pleasure of reading (or even seeing) your story, it has been respectfully declined.

Good luck finding publication elsewhere.

Best,

Editor

40

DROWNING

I WARN her not to over-water the plant in the window, but she insists that more water is needed to reach the roots. This is just like her: to do a little too much, to love a little too hard. Just like that plant, one day I, too, will drown.

THE DEATH OF THE MIXTAPE

HE REMEMBERED a time when mixtapes weren't about a rising emcee trying to attract a record label. Back in the day, a mixtape was something you spent the weekend compiling to give to someone you really liked. It was supposed to be the soundtrack for a romance in real time.

PROTEST IN THE TIME OF COVID

As the previous night's fires mixed with the morning fog, Alex put on his face mask and went out to retrieve his morning newspaper from the driveway. His street was quiet, peaceful, untouched. Inside his home, his wife and son slept upstairs, oblivious to the fire still raging within him.

43

NEO NEW JACK

THE KIDS WERE STILL ROCKING sneaker models from his childhood, the t-shirts and sweatshirts, too. They brought back the dance moves—and the New Jack Swing soundtrack to go along with it.

Like rap, it was never supposed to last, but oh, how wrong they turned out to be.

44

I'M STILL WAITING

PETE WAS the one who carried the boom box on the bus whenever the band took trips out of town. He always sat alone, making it his solemn duty to play slow jams on the long rides back. In the darkness, though, he could only imagine the others making out.

45

A KISS TO REMEMBER

THEIR FIRST KISS took place in the stairwell outside of the gymnasium at a basketball game. It was soft, brief, passionate, and both of them would be unable to stop reflecting over its beauty when they reluctantly returned to their seats to sit next to their dates for the evening.

46

SURREAL CARTOON

DURING THOSE SATURDAY mornings of summer, before trips to the mall to see and be seen, they whispered about girls they liked, wanted to step to but were too afraid to, wondering what ninth grade would be like and if they'd be noticed anymore. At least they had each other.

THE STEPFORD SNEAKERHEADS

EVERY BOY in the mall rocked a pair of retro Jordans, laces untied, pants tight, yet sagging, each a reflection of the other, all mirroring someone they'd seen on the Internet rocking the same thing, heads held high embodying the definition of "dope" as dictated to them by someone else.

PENTHOUSE PROPERTY ON CLOUD 9

HIS WORLD TILTED JUST a little more each time she walk by, her movements so smooth and fluid, as if on beat to a song he couldn't readily identify. By the time he realized it was Ne-Yo's "Champagne Life," she'd already turned his world upside down, like MJ kissing Spider-Man.

ACCEPTANCE

THE POETRY COLLECTION got the better of her for several years, as she wrote and rewrote pieces, workshopped them with her classmates, turned to an assorted list of recommended poets, and journaled her life. In the end, she discovered her authentic art only when she learned to accept herself completely.

THE CLOSING OF THE STRANGE MUSEUM

THE CURRENT GENERATION was decidedly boring, as it included largely well-adjusted writers who taught at prestigious universities and published collections and sought tenure. It'd abandoned many of the vices of the previous generations, eschewing anecdotes of wild, drunken debauchery and fantastic suicides. The future generation would be even more tame.

PART 2

51

THE ALTAR

THE PEOPLE GATHERED at the altar and left their problems there for a moment before lifting them and placing them back on their shoulders to walk away. It was like watching the hitman who poisoned the mark's drink, only to stir it with a finger and taste it by accident.

52

THE STRUGGLE

His GOAL WAS to write 1500 words a day toward his novel, and on many days he was able to hit his mark. On others, however, he found himself struggling to get even ten words onto the page, his outline taunting him like a Spanish matador waving an elegant muleta.

53

REUNION

THEY BOTH ARRIVED at the class reunion with their families in tow. They spoke to each other cordially, doing their best to imagine they were from a universe where there wasn't so much shared history, like this meeting didn't feel like the suppressed desire for one's favorite band to reunite.

54

BREATH

SOMETIMES HE WOULD LIE on his back in the bathtub, his face resting just beneath the surface of the water, holding his breath and counting. He wasn't training for anything in particular— he couldn't even swim— but somehow this felt like a survival skill he would surely one day need.

ON BEING PROFLIIC

SHE FEARED one day she would run out of ideas, that she'd been fortunate up till that point in her life to be so prolific. Each day as she sat down at her laptop, she would tap into that well, and, surprisingly, there was always something there, awaiting her command.

THE FIRST LOOK

THE PHOTOGRAPHER GUIDED him to the gazebo and told him to close his eyes. Standing in anticipation, he listened as she slowly ascended the stairs.

"Open your eyes," the photographer requested.

Everything that happened afterwards was a blur of emotions, but they'd always have the pictures to tell the story.

57

THE GAME

SHE EXPLAINED the rules to him this way:

"First, you drop your pants and pull on your winkie three times. Then, you chase me and try to touch me with it."

He didn't know whether to be disturbed by the rules or the fact she'd called this a "children's game."

58

LAUGHTER

His goal was to make her laugh, something he was prepared to work for indefinitely. At first he got polite chuckles for his efforts. Then a full laugh. Then she started snorting with her laughter. Finally, she peed on herself. He knew then to be careful what he wished for.

THE LETTER AFTER THE DEAR JOHN LETTER

LANCE,

I know I'm probably the last person you expected to hear from, but I accidentally left my Toni Morrison books on your shelves. I was hoping you could mail them to me at my cousin's house. I'll reimburse you for it. Again, sorry it didn't work out.

Best,

Danielle

60

THE SONG

SHE HAD A LOVE/HATE relationship with it: it'd been her biggest hit, one she'd written after he left her for Meredith (*she still remembered the name after all these years!*), but she'd grown so much since then.

Still, her fans would always hold her to that song, that memory.

THE VILLAGE OF A THOUSAND VENUSES

EACH YEAR, before harvest season, the villagers select one of their women to perform a heavily choreographed dance to satiate the Beast. If she is favored, the crops will be robust; if she fails, one of the men will be eaten by the Beast.

Clara trips on the first move.

THE QUEEN

EVEN WHEN SHURI WAS A SHORTY, her father had her knuckle-rapping beats on the kitchen table, freestyling in household cyphers. The dudes at school feared her. So did the industry. None of it stopped her from rocking the mic, though. She knew eventually they'd have to bow down to her.

63

BOYS AND GUNS

THE MEN TOLD the boys the guns were props—to show force. It was their constitutional right to have them and to protest their government.

They were disciplined and law-abiding.

They taught the boys how to safely handle, load, and fire them, but they swore they'd never actually use them.

THE STORY

FOR YEARS, he wrote hundreds of tiny stories, thinking each one a jewel until the next one came along. Story after story, collection after collection, he felt his plethora of pieces fail to gain traction, until one day a single story did. That story became the backbone of his reputation.

65

LOVE MEANS NOTHING

THEY CUDDLED under the lamps of the tennis court, trying not to think about their dorm curfews.

"I love you," he said, apropos of nothing.

She glanced away, uncomfortable.

He wanted to take it back, not because he didn't feel it, but because she didn't want it.

But he didn't.

THE VALUE OF ART

IT WAS ALLEGED he often slept on his paintings, paint sticking to his clothing, his hands, his face. Some collectors swore their pieces contained strands of his locs stuck to them. He was their wild child savant, darling of the art world. Now, all he had to do was die.

67

PURPLE
A PUBLISHING STORY

HE DIDN'T HAVE a title before he started, hoping it would come as he wrote the book. It didn't. By the time he finished the book, he was no closer to a title. He combed poems, quotes, album lyrics. Still nothing. He chose a color, and it became a bestseller.

VACATIONS IN THE 1980S

THE BOYS LOVED SUMMER VACATIONS. Their parents would pick cities far enough away that they'd need to leave out early in the morning, darkness surrounding the car between stretches of illuminated highway, Anita Baker playing on the tape in the cassette deck, the boys trying to sleep, giddy with anticipation.

69

A DIFFERENCE OF OPINION

CRITICS HATED HIS STORIES. Their biggest critique was the plots didn't have beginnings or endings. In fact, referring to them as plots was fairly generous. But he maintained the stories worked, that a story had something preceding and following it, regardless of where one decided to begin or end it.

73

WILTING UNDER THE DRAGON

NIECEE'S COUSIN had convinced her to go on the blind date. Now Niecee was struggling to hold her breath. Brad kept talking about himself, laughing at his own jokes. The food seemed to take forever to arrive. By the time it finally did, his breath had nearly melted her face.

71

THE GHOST

ONLY ARTHUR COULD SEE the outline of the girl standing by the window. He wanted to tell his parents, but he knew they wouldn't believe him.

Nancy saw the outline of the boy standing by the door. She wanted to tell her parents, but she knew they wouldn't believe her.

BRAID MY HAIR

CHRIS LEANED back between Tonya's thighs, resting his back on the porch steps. She gently parted his hair with a long-tail comb and carefully twisted the oiled pieces of his hair into neat plaits. They'd always been friends, but in that moment he wondered if maybe they could be more.

THE UNFINISHED JOURNAL

THE JOURNAL NAIMA discovered at the used book table in the square contained multiple entries by different people. With at least fifty pages remaining, she thought it would be fun to finish it out.

When the journal reached the table again, Naima had managed ten pages before her unfortunate accident.

DANCING BY MOONLIGHT

AT NIGHT she dances to their favorite song, imagining his fingers interlocked with hers, his arm sweeping around her waist. Her hips aren't what they used to be and her movements are slow, but the music guides her sweetly, her memories of him filling in every space between the beats.

MAKING THE GRASS GREENER

THEY SPENT an enormous amount of time making the new planet inhabitable. It represented a clean start, a chance to get everything right this time around. What they didn't realize, though, was that there'd be impossibilities ahead—and that it would've been much easier to simply fix their home planet.

THE LAST NOVEL

As HE CRAFTED each word carefully into what would become his last novel, he considered announcing to his readers that he had planned to retire from writing, but thought against it. Doing such a thing was akin to marketing, making a spectacle of one's self. He would simply stop writing.

77

THE MINIMALIST

HE OWNED THREE SHIRTS, three pairs of underwear, three pairs of socks, two pairs of pants, three pairs of shoes, a hoodie, three baseball caps, a cable sweater, a parka, a blazer, and an automatic watch. He once owned much more—back before he became a millionaire. Oh, the ironies.

78

MOVING ON

THE MUSE ARRIVED at his desk late one morning with news she would no longer be able to meet with him at their appointed time. It was crushing news, as he'd come to rely on her to get his work done. She apologized but told him others needed her more.

ONE OF A MILLION SMALL DEATHS
OR HOW MY PSEUDONYM SLAYED ME

LAQUESHA DIDN'T HATE "ALICE." In fact, she tried not to feel anything. A job was a job. It shouldn't matter who got the credit. The publisher had more faith in "Alice" than in "LaQuesha." The objective, after all, was to sell books.

It would be the first of many compromises.

THE GREAT AMERICAN NOVELLA

THE ORIGINAL PLAN was to write the Great American novel, at least 250,000 words, but every time Victor began to write it, it came out in tiny pieces. He refused to accept that his book was really a novella, so he tinkered with it for the rest of his life.

81

DIALOGUE

"Have you ever noticed the amount of dialogue in a Tarantino film?"

"Yep. It's normally on some random shit, too."

"Like people talking about foot massages or cheeseburgers."

"Yep. Think they'd let a Black director get away with all of that shit?"

"Not really. But maybe a Black microfictionist could."

CHOOSE YOUR OWN ADVENTURE

COLE PASSES by a phone booth doubling as a time machine on 3rd Avenue.

1. If he acknowledges it, this story is *Afrosurrealistic*.

2. If he gets in and goes to the future, this story is *Afrofuturistic*.

3. If he never notices it, there'd be nothing special about this story.

83

STEAM

THEY PAINTED their naked bodies orange with black stripes across their backs and bottoms. Some crawled around on all fours, while others sat on stools inside their cages.

It was a scientific experiment to some and performance art to others.

The grant covered them both, viewing this as interdepartmental collaboration.

84

MASQUERADE

THE LOWER HALVES of their faces were covered with KN95 masks, the upper halves of their faces covered with colorfully adorned masquerade masks, their bodies cloaked within oversized black clothing.

They danced without an idea of the other's actual appearance, talking and sharing, falling for each other in this masquerade.

85

SUMMERTIME

OR HOW GLOBAL WARMING SPOILED EVERYTHING

As a child, he'd loved summers, the sun beaming over his small town, the clouds drifting across the Smurf-blue sky. Dripping popsicles. Cookouts. Birthday parties. Winks from the girl next door.

As an adult, he hated summers, the sweltering, torturous heat, relentlessly wrapping itself around him.

He'd outgrown everything else.

HARRY NILSSON HAD IT ALL WRONG
OR ONE IS A BEAUTIFUL NUMBER

FOR MUCH OF HER LIFE, Sharice feared being alone. She was made to feel she needed a companion to be complete. This resulted in many missteps.

As she grew older, though, she came to understand she was enough all by herself and didn't require anyone to co-sign on her dreams.

A FAIRYTALE FOR DISGRUNTLED WRITERS

ONCE UPON A TIME, a writer wrote a book and the book bombed.

The publisher barely promoted it, and nobody bought it.

Afterwards, no other publishers would touch his work, since his sales were bad.

He nearly gave up writing, but he didn't.

He kept right on writing.

The end.

88

THE READING

HE LEFT the reading wondering if he had possibly given away something in his body language or if he had inadvertently given off some kind of clue about his life. He harbored a healthy skepticism, but the medium had been right about so many things.

Still, he refused to believe.

89

BURIED TREASURE

THE OLD MAN WHISPERED, his voice barely audible. His three adult sons leaned in closer.

"The gold," he started, pausing to catch his breath. "The gold is buried behind the …."

"Dad?" the oldest said, but he, like the others, knew the old man was gone—and with it their hopes.

ONE OF THE SONGS IN HER VAULT

SHE WROTE a song about a woman writing a song about a woman writing a song, but she never recorded it, feeling the song too meta, too personal (in an indirect way), and she feared no one would ever understand what the song was supposed to be about, including herself.

91

THE END OF A SITUATION

WHEN HE BROUGHT her the bouquet of roses, she knew she'd have to end it. Their situation was one of convenience—of pleasure—where no feelings were supposed to be involved. There were no "I love you's" or "Have sweet dreams" in their situation, and there definitely weren't any roses.

FIFTY BOOKS

HIS GOAL WAS to shrink his library of thousands of books to just fifty. His fellow bibliophiles questioned his sanity, but he insisted the minimalism of his collection was necessary to bring greater focus in his life. They disagreed—mainly because they couldn't figure out how to do that themselves.

93

THE ART OF SNEAKER COLLECTING
OR HOW I STOPPED FOLLOWING HYPEBEASTS

HE STARTED his sneaker collection by buying as many Jordan 1's as he could, in every possible colorway. Over time, his collection expanded into other models and brands, and he eventually learned his own tastes. Those Jordan 1's were the first of the collection he'd eventually sell off.

THE DEATH OF A VAMPIRE

WHEN THE AUTOPSY for the vampire was officially completed, all of the writers, whether local, national, or international, gathered around the medical examiner, their curiosity of Mt. Everest proportions.

The medical examiner, holding a megaphone in one hand and the results in the other, said, "This vampire died of clichés."

HIS UNCLE'S JOURNALS
AFTER ROALD DAHL

THE UNCLE HAD LEFT a box of his journals, filled with escapades of traveling and romancing women around the world, to his great-nephew, who upon opening the box, searched through each of the journals and frowned, as he could not read a single page, being that he never learned cursive.

MS. JOHNSON NAMES HER FIRSTBORN

SHE HAD HEARD the word before, but had never bothered to look it up. It sounded nice and rolled off the tongue easily. Few words could dance around in a person's mouth like this one, so when she gave birth to her son, she, without hesitation, named him Fellatio Johnson.

THROW PILLOWS

"THROW PILLOWS ARE A SHAM."

"Nice double entendre."

"I mean it. You keep buying them and buying them, trying to balance each side of the sofa. In the end, you can't even see the sofa for all the throw pillows! It's a racket, I tell you."

"No, it's a sham."

WHAT HE LEFT BEHIND

WHEN THEY FINALLY CAME FOR him, the small boat they'd brought to carry him to the other side couldn't hold more than himself. The things he'd spent decades collecting, cultivating, curating, would have to remain behind.

As he sailed across the surface, he suddenly questioned how he'd spent his life.

DREAMS OF SPACE

THE KIDS at Bria's school made fun of her for wearing an astronaut helmet. Her grandmother'd taught her about faith, though. If it was sunny but you had faith it'd rain, you stepped outside with the umbrella opened. One day Bria would go to space, regardless of what others thought.

LIGHTSPEED

SHE STARED AT HIM, admiring his physique and his dark complexion. She knew, without question, she would take him home with her.

He, on the other hand, knew if she ever asked him, he would go anywhere she wanted to go.

After all, he'd never been on a spaceship before.

ACKNOWLEDGMENTS

"Reunion," "Seeds," "Euphonic Cacophony," "Drowning," "Beaufort," "Cotton Candy Clouds," "Protest in the Time of Covid," "Able to Leap Tall Insecurities in a Single Bound," "Men in Mourning," "The Ghost," and "The Bibliophile" were published in *50-Word Stories*.

Thank you to my two biggest cheerleaders, Elle and Zoë; The Walker & Holbrook & Maxie & Whittley & Williams families; the Dumas Collective; the James River Writers; the staff at *Writer's Digest*; the Indie Author Project; Worldspark Studios; and the Hampton University Department of English and Foreign Languages.

ALSO BY RAN WALKER

B-Sides and Remixes

30 Love: A Novel

Mojo's Guitar: A Novel / (Il était une fois Morris Jones)

Afro Nerd in Love: A Novella

The Keys of My Soul: A Novel

The Race of Races: A Novel

The Illest: A Novella

Bessie, Bop, or Bach: Collected Stories

Four Floors (with Sabin Prentis)

Black Hand Side: Stories

White Pages: A Novel

She Lives in My Lap

Reverb

Work-In-Progress

Daykeeper

Most of My Heroes Don't Appear On No Stamps

Portable Black Magic: Tales of the Afro Strange

The Strange Museum: 50-Word Stories

Bees + Things + Flowers: Microfictions

The World Is Yours: Microfictions

Can I Kick It?: Sneaker Microfiction and Poetry

The Golden Book: A 50-Year Marriage Told In 50-Word Stories

Keep It 100: 100-Word Stories

ABOUT THE AUTHOR

Ran Walker (he/him) is the author of twenty-nine books. His short stories, flash fiction, microfiction, and poetry have appeared in a variety of anthologies and journals. Prior to becoming a writer and educator, he worked in magazine publishing and practiced law in Mississippi.

He is the winner of the Indie Author Project's 2019 National Indie Author of the Year Award (selected by judges from *Library Journal*, *Publishers Weekly*, IngramSpark, St. Martin's Press, and *Writer's Digest*), the 2019 Black Caucus of the American Library Association Best Fiction Ebook Award, the 2018 Virginia Indie Author Project Award for Adult Fiction, and the 2021 Blind Corner Afrofuturism Microfiction Contest. Ran is an Assistant Professor of English and Creative Writing at Hampton University and teaches with Writer's Digest University. He lives in Virginia with his wife and much better half, Lauren, and his amazing daughter, Zoë.

CPSIA information can be obtained
at www.ICGtesting.com
Printed in the USA
BVHW012039140223
658501BV00019B/332

9 781020 001383